I0519426

The Bahamian Tempest

The Angelina Novellas

Camille Laurent

Copyright

Introducing Angelina Rossi

Angelina is a striking Italian woman of thirty-eight, with shoulder-length dark brown hair that catches golden highlights in the sun, and warm amber eyes that hint at deeper mysteries. Her olive-toned skin speaks of her Mediterranean heritage, and her classically beautiful features—high cheekbones, full lips, and an expressive face—effortlessly convey both warmth and determination. Years of physical farm work have given her a graceful, athletic build, and her elegant hands bear the honest calluses of labor, a testament to her connection to the earth. While at her Tuscan olive farm, she typically favors simple, well-made clothing like linen shirts, fitted jeans, and leather boots. However, during her escapes to her private retreat on Necker Island, she transforms, embracing flowing sundresses and a more uninhibited style.

Angelina possesses a magnetic warmth that naturally draws people to her, yet beneath this inviting exterior lies an inner strength forged by years of managing both land and legacy. She is fiercely passionate about life's authentic pleasures: the exquisite taste of perfectly pressed olive oil, the grounding feel of rich soil between her fingers, and the profound intimacy of connections with those she truly trusts. Her sensual nature is not merely physical; it extends to a deep appreciation for beauty in all forms. She is fiercely protective of her privacy and family traditions, often speaking in measured tones that further hint at the complexities within. Her loving nature, while selective, is profound, and she maintains a strong libido, viewing her sexuality as an integral part of her vitality and connection to life itself. She is selective but passionate in her romantic encounters, preferring quality over quantity and maintaining the same exacting standards for lovers as she did for her world-renowned olive oil – only the finest will do.

Born into a generations-old olive farming family in Tuscany, Angelina inherited the farm after her father's passing when she was thirty-five. Through shrewd business decisions and unwavering dedication to quality, she transformed the modest operation into a premium olive oil brand sought after by exclusive restaurants worldwide. Her success allowed her to purchase her private retreat on Necker Island, where she escapes the demands of her public life and the constraints of small-town gossip. Lately, however, even her island sanctuary couldn't fully silence the mounting anxieties from home. A new, aggressive competitor was encroaching on her market, threatening not just her profits, but the very legacy her family had built. She had never married, often claiming she was "wed to the land," though whispers suggested she had

had passionate affairs with carefully chosen lovers who understood and respected her need for discretion.

Angelina's journey, as explored in these novellas, involves learning to balance her fierce independence with the challenging act of allowing others into her closely guarded world. As external pressures threaten her farm's legacy, she must decide whether to fight alone or trust others with her deepest secrets. Her character arc explores the tension between protecting what she has meticulously built and opening herself to new possibilities that could either destroy or elevate everything she holds dear. This story is an adventure, a celebration of "The Good Life," told with a tone that is often secretive, always alluring.

Chapter 1: The Azure Invitation

Angelina stepped onto the sun-drenched deck of her Bahamian mansion, the morning breeze a warm caress against her olive-toned skin. Below, the turquoise waters stretched endlessly, a shimmering expanse of sapphire and emerald that promised infinite possibilities, a stark contrast to the ordered rows of olive trees she knew so well. This was her sanctuary, a private retreat on Necker Island, a world away from the ancient groves of Tuscany. Even here, the faint scent of cypress and rich earth, carried on an imagined breeze, would sometimes remind her of home. Yet, the rigid constraints of her small village life and the gnawing anxieties of her business back home occasionally intruded. Her phone, clutched in her elegant hand, vibrated with a new email from Marco, her farm manager. Another aggressive move by a competitor – a predatory price drop on a key distributor. The knot in her stomach tightened, a familiar clenching that even the Bahamian sun couldn't fully melt. She sighed, a soft exhalation that carried the weight of her legacy. *Here*, she reminded herself, *here the burdens fade. Here, I am free.* This island was where her strong libido, a force as natural and essential as breathing, found its truest, most uninhibited expression. She was a different woman here – bolder, more uninhibited, perpetually in pursuit of experiences that stirred her very soul.

Her gaze swept across the pristine crescent of white sand, landing on a figure emerging from the waves. He was a vision, a force of nature, all raw power and untamed energy. Sun-bleached white hair, a dramatic contrast against his deeply tanned skin, clung to his forehead, and his eyes, a striking deep ocean blue, held an intense, wild spark. He moved with the effortless grace of a creature born of the sea, his muscular, well-defined physique glistening with droplets of seawater, each ripple of muscle a testament to years spent battling currents and exploring hidden depths. He carried himself with the confidence of someone completely at home in the water, a man whose very being seemed shaped by the ocean's vastness. His name, she would soon learn, was Kai. Kai Oceanus, a name that perfectly suited the professional free diver and ocean exploration guide.

As he strode towards her, the sand crunching softly under his bare feet, Angelina's heart quickened. A familiar yet intensely potent longing bloomed within her chest—a longing that whispered promises of depths of passion yet unexplored. This wasn't the first time she'd seen him. For the past few years, their visits to the Bahamas had consistently overlapped, a delightful coincidence that had led to a series of pleasant, casual encounters. They'd exchanged light banter at local fish fries, shared a laugh over a spilled drink at a beach bar, and even found themselves discussing their backgrounds at small island gatherings. She knew he was a free diver; he knew about her Tuscan olive farm, but they never exchanged their names. He called her "farmer and she called him "diver." It was a funny game they played with each other. There had always been an undeniable current of attraction between them, a silent acknowledgment in their lingering gazes, but neither had ever acted on it. It was a comfortable, unspoken tension, a tantalizing "what if" that had always remained just out of reach. Until now.

He stopped a few feet from the deck, his gaze direct and unwavering, a slow, confident smile spreading across his lips. "Good morning," his voice, deep and resonant, washed over her, like the gentle lapping of the waves against the shore. "I'm Kai. Kai Oceanus. I saw you up here and couldn't resist introducing myself formally. This view is almost as captivating as you are." The words were bold, yet his eyes held a genuine warmth that disarmed her. A spark of recognition danced in his own eyes, confirming her unspoken thought.

Angelina felt a mischievous smile curve her own full lips, a playful challenge in her warm amber eyes. "Almost?" she purred, her voice a sultry invitation, a subtle shift from the measured tones she used back home. "A bold claim, considering the majesty of the Bahamian sea." She descended the few steps from the deck to the sand, her bare feet sinking slightly into the warm grains. "I'm Angelina. And I confess, your emergence from the waves was quite the spectacle. Like a myth made real." Her magnetic warmth, a natural allure that drew people to her, was fully engaged, a silent invitation for him to step closer. "I remember your stories about diving. It is clearly your passion. I enjoyed listening to your adventures. I even considered taking diving lessons, but never got around to it."

Kai chuckled, a rich, genuine sound that resonated deep in his chest. "The ocean and I have a very intimate relationship. It tends to bring out my truest self," he said, his voice deep and resonant. "It's where I feel most free." His striking blue eyes, now closer, held a knowing glint, as if he saw beyond her polished exterior to the wildness she usually kept hidden. "And something tells me, Angelina, that you understand that kind of freedom. A freedom that goes beyond land, beyond expectations. Beyond, perhaps, the weight of an olive farm? And yes," he added, his gaze holding hers, "I remember. Brief glimpses. Always a mystery. But this time feels different, doesn't it?"

"More than you know," she replied, her voice holding a measured tone that hinted at deeper mysteries, as she closed the distance between them. Her elegant hands, showing the honest calluses of labor from years on her olive farm, almost instinctively trailed along his broad, wet chest, feeling the warmth of his skin, the tautness of his muscles beneath her touch. A jolt, primal and undeniable, passed between them. Their mouths met in a feverish kiss, tasting the salt of the sea on their lips, a raw, uninhibited exchange that spoke of unspoken words, of a connection that needed no explanation. It was a kiss that promised adventure, a prelude to the awakening she knew was brewing, a testament to her selective yet profound loving nature. The scent of his sun-warmed skin, mingled with the clean tang of the ocean, filled her senses, a potent elixir.

Kai's hands roamed, caressing her curves, igniting a fire that only he seemed capable of quenching. "Let me show you how much I'm drawn to that wildness," he murmured against her skin, his breath sending delicious shivers down her spine. His voice held a hint of his inherent dominance, a quiet command. "I know a spot, just beyond those palms, where the world melts away." His eyes held a silent question, a challenge she was eager to accept.

Without waiting for a formal invitation, she took his hand, her fingers intertwining with his, their skin already accustomed to the feel of each other. The sun was climbing higher, painting the sky in shades of brilliant blue, but a secluded daybed, nestled under a canopy of swaying palm fronds, offered a tempting escape from its intensity. The air was heavy with the intoxicating scent of blooming frangipani and the endless, salty kiss of the ocean. As they surrendered to their desires, the rhythmic sound of the waves crashing against the shore became the primal beat of their unfolding passion, a true taste of "The Good Life."

Chapter 2: Daybed Delights

They tumbled onto the plush cushions of the daybed, the soft fabric yielding beneath their weight. Kai's eyes, dark with desire, devoured her, a silent appreciation that made Angelina's skin prickle with anticipation. He wasn't just a man who appreciated beauty; he was a man whose gaze felt like a warm current, pulling her deeper into a world where only sensation mattered. Her sensual nature responded eagerly to his unspoken admiration, a silent affirmation that only the finest experiences, like the finest olive oil, truly satisfied her.

"I forgot how stunning you are up close," Kai whispered, his fingers deftly unbuttoning the lightweight linen shirt she wore over her bikini. His touch was light, almost reverent, yet held an undercurrent of urgency, a subtle assertion of his intent. "Every curve, every line... a masterpiece." The subtle scent of his skin, a mix of sun, salt, and something uniquely masculine, filled her nostrils, intoxicating her.

Angelina laughed softly, a playful glint in her eyes. "And you, Kai, are quite the sculpture yourself. All hard lines and raw power." Her hands mirrored his, tracing the defined muscles of his chest, feeling the tautness of his abdomen, a silent conversation between their bodies.

Their clothes quickly became unnecessary barriers. The linen shirt, her bikini top, his swim trunks – they were shed with an urgent clumsiness, discarded onto the warm sand around the daybed. Their naked bodies, kissed by the sun and cooled by the gentle breeze, pressed together, skin against skin, a symphony of sensation. The taste of salt lingered on their lips from their earlier kiss, a primal reminder of their wild connection.

Angelina's soft moans filled the air as Kai's skilled hands and mouth began their exploration. He started with her lips, a deep, lingering kiss that left her breathless, then trailed a path down her neck, tasting the lingering salt on her skin, eliciting shivers that danced across her shoulders. His tongue flicked over her collarbone, then descended to her breasts, suckling one taut nipple until it hardened exquisitely, then moving to the other, teasing and tormenting her with equal fervor. A faint, sweet scent of frangipani, carried on the breeze, mingled with the rising heat of their bodies.

"Oh, Kai," she gasped, her fingers threading through his sun-kissed hair, holding him close, urging him deeper into the pleasure. "You know exactly what to do." Her voice was a raw whisper, far removed from the composed tones she used in business meetings.

He chuckled against her skin, a low, rumbling sound. "It's instinct, Angelina. Your body sings to me." His hands roamed lower, tracing the curve of her waist, the flare of her hips, before delving between her thighs. His fingers found her wetness, stroking and circling her most sensitive spot, eliciting a gasp that turned into a moan. The soft brush of the daybed fabric against her bare skin, the gentle sway of the palm fronds above, all contributed to the heightened sensory experience.

Angelina arched her back, offering herself more fully to his touch, her hips instinctively rising to meet his probing fingers. The pleasure was a hot, insistent wave, building with every stroke, every kiss. She felt herself unraveling, her control slipping away, replaced by a delicious surrender. A fleeting, almost phantom thought of Marco's email, of the tight control she usually maintained over her business, flickered and vanished in the face of this raw, uninhibited freedom. Here, the olive groves and the encroaching competitor felt a lifetime away.

"I want you inside me, Kai," she panted, her voice thick with desire. "Now." The demand was primal, a stark contrast to the careful negotiations she usually engaged in.

He pulled back just enough to look into her eyes, a triumphant smirk on his lips. "As you wish, my tempest." His words held the weight of a man accustomed to leading, to taking charge.

With a smooth, powerful thrust, he entered her, filling her completely. Angelina cried out, her head falling back against the cushions as pure, unadulterated pleasure washed over her. Kai began to move, his hips snapping forward with urgent need, their bodies creating a primal rhythm. Angelina reveled in his impressive size, a perfect fit for her own boundless desires, a sensation that anchored her to the moment, silencing the last whispers of her responsibilities.

The daybed creaked with the rhythm of their lovemaking, a symphony of desire and longing. Their breaths came in ragged gasps, mingling with the soft slaps of skin against skin. The sun, now high in the sky, cast dappled patterns through the palm fronds, illuminating their entwined forms. The salty tang of the ocean air, the subtle sweetness of her own arousal, and the earthy scent of the warm sand created a heady perfume around them.

In the aftermath of their intimate dance, as their breathing slowed and their bodies still hummed with the echoes of pleasure, Angelina and Kai found solace in each other's arms. The daybed, now bearing the marks of their passion, provided a temporary haven from the outside world.

"I could stay lost in you forever," Kai whispered, his lips brushing her ear, his voice husky with contentment.

Angelina smiled, a soft, contented smile. "Then stay. Indulge with me a while longer. We have all the time in the world here, and so much more to explore." She pushed away the lingering thought of Marco's email, choosing to fully immerse herself in the moment, a luxury she rarely afforded herself back in Tuscany, where every hour was accounted for, every decision weighed against the farm's future. The contrast was stark, and deliciously liberating.

Their fingers entwined, and they shared a look that spoke volumes—a silent agreement to prolong their erotic adventure, to delve deeper into the uninhibited freedom the island offered.

Chapter 3: Bioluminescent Secrets

As the sun began its slow descent, painting the sky with hues of fiery pink, molten orange, and deep violet, Angelina and Kai, still naked, moved from the daybed to the crystal-clear waters. The warm ocean lapped at their skin, a gentle balm cooling the lingering heat that still simmered between them. The air was thick with the scent of salt and the promise of a magical evening. Angelina felt a lightness she rarely experienced in the structured world of her Tuscan farm, where every decision, every harvest, was weighed with generations of tradition. Here, the only tradition was the unfolding moment.

Kai captured Angelina's hand, his grip firm and reassuring, leading her further out, where the water danced with the vibrant hues of the setting sun. "I want to show you something," he said, his eyes alight with a playful, mysterious spark. "A place few ever see. A secret I share only with the ocean, and now, you." His voice held a quiet intimacy, a subtle invitation to a deeper level of trust, a rare glimpse into his emotionally guarded self.

Angelina, intrigued by the secret in his voice and the anticipation in his eyes, followed willingly. The water grew deeper, enveloping them in its embrace, and the last rays of sunlight stretched across the surface, turning the ocean into a liquid canvas. The thought of secrets, of guarded places, reminded her of her own closely held world back home, the private anxieties about the encroaching competitor, the constant need to protect her family's legacy. This openness, this willingness to share a hidden part of his world, felt like a profound gift.

He guided her along a hidden path through a cluster of ancient, moss-covered rocks, a narrow passage barely wide enough for two. The air grew cooler, damper, and the sounds of the open ocean faded, replaced by the gentle drip of water within the enclosed space. Then, they emerged into a hidden cove, a secret spot known only to local divers and, apparently, Kai.

The water within the cove glowed with a soft, ethereal bioluminescence, a shimmering, otherworldly light that pulsed with every movement. Tiny, microscopic organisms ignited with a ghostly blue-green light, turning the dark water into a living, breathing constellation. "It's like a dream," she whispered, her voice hushed with wonder, turning to him, her eyes reflecting the magical glow. "A secret world." The cool, damp air on her skin, the subtle scent of damp rock and living water, heightened the surreal beauty of the place.

"It is our world, Angelina," Kai murmured, his voice a low rumble in the enclosed space. "A world where we can be whoever we want to be. Where inhibitions melt away and the extraordinary becomes ordinary." He paused, his gaze thoughtful. "This island holds secrets. And it asks for trust. Like the ocean asks for trust when you dive deep into her. You've built your life on tradition, on careful cultivation, haven't you? But here, it's about letting go, about trusting the unknown." His words, though gentle, touched on the core of her internal conflict – the push and pull between the structured world of her farm and the boundless freedom she found here. It also hinted at his own journey of learning to trust and be vulnerable.

His hands found her waist, pulling her close under the water's surface, their bodies fitting together perfectly. The bioluminescent water, warm and inviting, lapped at their skin, enhancing the sensation of every touch. Their kisses were fierce and hungry, a stark contrast to the serene, mystical beauty of their surroundings, yet perfectly aligned with the wildness that now thrummed between them. The taste of his skin, mingled with the faint, metallic tang of the glowing water, was unlike anything she had ever experienced.

As their lips parted, Angelina gasped for breath, her eyes sparkling with delight, reflecting the shimmering water. "This place is magical, Kai. Truly magical. I feel like we've stumbled into a realm of pure fantasy." The idea of pure fantasy, of stepping outside the rigid reality of her life, felt incredibly liberating, a stark departure from the constant vigilance required to protect her family's olive oil legacy.

Kai's smile was mischievous in the soft, pulsing light. "Fantasy and reality often blend in the right company, my love." His hands, now roaming her back, savored the feel of her skin, slick with saltwater and desire. Angelina's fingers trailed along Kai's strong shoulders, down his back, savoring the feel of his powerful physique, the subtle flex of his muscles.

Their passion ignited once more, fueled by the intoxicating atmosphere. They moved in sync, their kisses and touches becoming more urgent, more demanding. The ancient grotto, with its cool limestone walls and hidden depths, provided the perfect backdrop for their erotic dance, a stage for their unbridled desires. The rhythmic sound of their bodies moving in the water, the soft splashes, created a natural symphony.

The sound of the gentle waves, now a distant murmur, echoed around them, creating a natural rhythm to which their bodies moved.

Angelina's soft cries of pleasure mingled with the rush of the ocean, a symphony of nature and desire. Kai's skilled hands and mouth knew exactly how to arouse her, sending waves of pleasure coursing through her body, making her tremble. The faint, earthy smell of the damp rock mingled with the clean scent of the ocean and the rising heat of their bodies.

As their passion built, the bioluminescent water illuminated their every move, casting an otherworldly light on their entwined forms. Their skin glowed, reflecting the phosphorescence, as if they were part of the sea itself, mythical creatures in a hidden paradise.

Chapter 4: Grotto's Embrace

Angelina's fingers curled around Kai's broad shoulders, and she pulled him close, their lips fused in a fiery kiss that tasted of salt and raw longing. With a surge of strength that surprised them both, she spun them around, pressing him against the cool, damp rock face of the grotto, asserting a new kind of power.

"Angelina," Kai breathed, his eyes gleaming with desire, a hint of surprise in his voice. "You have a wildness in you that matches my own, and a strength I find utterly intoxicating. I didn't know you had this side."

She smiled, her eyes glittering with a mischievous light, her body pressed flush against his. "You bring it out in me, Kai. You make me want to explore every facet of my desires. Now, let me show you what else I can do." The sensation of taking control, of asserting her will, felt profoundly different from the constant defensive stance she adopted in her business dealings.

Her hands roamed freely, exploring his sculpted body with a newfound confidence, trailing down his chest, and lower, eliciting a sharp intake of breath from him. She claimed his mouth again, her kisses demanding and insistent, tasting the salt on his skin, then moving to his neck, his jawline, leaving a trail of fire.

Kai surrendered to her lead, his hands reaching up to tangle in her hair, holding her close as she took charge. Angelina's touch was confident and bold, knowing exactly how to arouse him, how to push his boundaries. Every caress, every kiss, was a deliberate stroke of passion, driving him to the peak of pleasure, making him tremble under her touch.

The grotto echoed with the sounds of their desire, the soft splash of water, their moans, and the rhythmic beat of the ocean outside. The contrast of the cool rock against their heated skin only added to the intensity of the moment, a delicious friction.

As Angelina's exploration became more fervent, Kai's breath quickened, his body growing taut with anticipation. "You're driving me wild," he managed to whisper, his voice hoarse with need, a plea in his eyes.

Angelina's fingers traced lazy patterns on Kai's skin, her touch light and teasing. She explored every inch of him, learning his body, knowing exactly how to push him to the brink. Her mouth followed suit, placing soft kisses along his collarbone, down his chest, and over his taut stomach, her tongue circling his navel before dipping lower.

Kai, breathless and desperate, whispered against her hair, "You're torturing me, Angelina. I'm at your mercy."

She just chuckled, a low, seductive sound that sent shivers through him. "Not yet, my love. I want you to burn for me. I want to savor every gasp, every tremor." The power of this control, so different from the exhausting battles with her competitor, was intoxicating.

The sound of the ocean, crashing against the rocks just outside the grotto, seemed to echo their escalating desire. The cool, damp grotto walls surrounded them, adding to the raw, primal atmosphere, a hidden chamber for their secret pleasures.

As Kai squirmed beneath her touch, Angelina relished the power she held over him. She took delight in his every reaction, his every plea, knowing that she held the key to his release, prolonging the exquisite agony.

"You like that, don't you?" she murmured, her lips brushing his ear, a triumphant smirk on her face.

Kai could only manage a nod, his body thrumming with anticipation, his eyes closed in surrender.

Angelina, sensing Kai's desire, positions him against the grotto wall, their bodies still slick with saltwater, the bioluminescent glow casting their forms in an ethereal light. With a confident smile, she takes charge, assuming a dominant stance, her eyes blazing with a newfound power.

"You want me to take you, Kai? To claim you as mine?" She teases, her voice low and husky, a sensual challenge.

Kai's eyes smolder with raw need, his breath coming in ragged gasps. "Yes, Angelina. Take me. I am yours. His words, a clear indication of his submissive side in intimate relationships, were a revelation.

She pushes him gently, positioning his hands against the rock for support. Then, with a deliberate, unhurried move, she steps forward, pressing her body against his, their heat merging. With a confident hand, she reaches between their bodies, guiding his impressive hardness to her entrance.

As she begins to move, her rhythm is slow and deliberate, building the tension with each thrust, each slow grind. Kai, spurred on by her assertive display, urges her on, his hips instinctively thrusting back against hers.

"Fuck me, Angelina. Claim me," he demands, his voice raw with desire, a desperate plea. "Harder. Faster."

Angelina obliges, her movements becoming more forceful, more relentless. She sets a fierce pace, her hips moving in a steady, powerful rhythm, their bodies creating a symphony of skin slapping against skin, echoing off the grotto walls.

Kai, caught in a whirlwind of sensations, surrenders completely to her, his breath coming in sharp gasps, his body trembling. "Harder, Angelina. I'm close. So close."

She leans in, her lips brushing his ear, her breath hot against his skin. "Come for me, Kai. Let go. Let me feel your release inside me."

Her words, coupled with the intense, relentless stimulation, push Kai over the edge. He cries out, his release claiming him with an intense, shuddering pleasure as Angelina continues her relentless thrusts, drawing out his ecstasy, milking every last drop of his climax.

As their passion peaks, their bodies shine in the bioluminescent glow, their skin gleaming with a layer of perspiration, a testament to their shared exertion. Angelina feels his warmth, his pulsing release deep within her, a profound connection forged in the heart of the grotto.

Chapter 5: The Pleasure Chamber's Whisper

Angelina and Kai, their bodies still humming with the afterglow of their grotto escapade, emerged into the cool night air, the moon now a silent sentinel in the vast Bahamian sky. Hand in hand, they made their way back to the mansion, their steps light, their minds already plotting the next indulgence.

"That was... transcendent," Kai murmured, his voice still a little hoarse, as they reached the sprawling main house. "You truly are a force of nature, Angelina." The hint of surprise in his voice suggested he hadn't fully anticipated her dominant side.

She squeezed his hand, a triumphant smirk playing on her lips. "And you, Kai, are a magnificent storm. But I have a feeling we've only just begun to explore the depths of our combined desires." Her eyes, dark and alluring, held a new kind of mischief. "There's something else I want to show you. A different kind of sanctuary. One I've been waiting to share with the right person." The thought of her Tuscan farm, of the heavy responsibility she carried, felt distant and almost irrelevant in this moment of blissful anticipation.

Kai's curiosity was immediately piqued. "Lead the way, my siren."

She led him not to her opulent bedroom, but to a discreet, almost hidden door at the far end of the mansion's sprawling basement. As she unlocked it, a faint, musky scent, mingled with something metallic and sweet, drifted out. The air was cooler down here, almost hushed.

They stepped into a space that was both surprising and utterly captivating. It was a custom-made, formal BDSM dungeon, a sanctuary of polished leather, gleaming metal, and soft, strategically placed lighting. Angelina had designed and built it herself over the past year, a secret project, waiting for the perfect partner to unlock its potential. Restraints of various materials and other implements of pleasure, each piece a silent invitation to explore. The bed, a massive, four-poster, dominated the room, its posts draped with leather and latex, and a plush chaise lounge chair, promising endless possibilities.

"This is my personal sanctuary," Angelina explained, her voice laced with promise, her eyes never leaving his. "I built this place, but I've been waiting for someone truly special to share its secrets with. This was a space of her own making, free from the prying eyes and judgments of her village, a place where the rules of the olive oil market held no sway.

Kai's eyes widened as he took in the scene, a gasp escaping his lips. "Angelina," he breathed, a mixture of awe and pleasant surprise in his voice. "This is... incredible. You truly are full of surprises." The very air seemed to spark with erotic possibility, a perfect match for his own hidden desires for control and intimacy.

"Let's play a sensual game." Angelina suggested, her eyes glittering with mischief as she gestured to a small, velvet-covered table beside the bed, where an ornate box rested.

Intrigued, Kai nodded, his pulse quickening. "What kind of game, my tempest?"

Angelina's smile widened as she produced a pair of beautifully crafted, multi-sided dice from the ornate box. One die had various body parts etched onto its faces (e.g., "lips," "neck," "thighs," "breasts," "cock," "cunt," "ass"), while the other had actions (e.g., "kiss," "lick," "suck," "tease," "bite," "spank," "massage"). "This, my dear Kai," she explained, her voice a low, seductive rumble, "This is the Game of Sensual Dice. We'll take turns rolling the dice. The combination dictates the pleasure. The person who rolls chooses who performs the action, and the other submits.

Kai's lips curved into a wicked smile. "I'm game, Angelina. Let the fun begin. I have a feeling this will be a very long night."

Angelina went first, her fingers trembling slightly with anticipation as she reached into the box. She rolled the dice. The first die landed on "thighs," and the second on "tease." "Ah, the thighs and tease," she purred, her eyes locking onto Kai's. "I choose... to tease your inner thighs."

Kai chuckled, a low, rumbling sound that sent a delightful shiver down her spine. "My pleasure, my dominatrix." He stretched out on the plush cushions, offering his legs.

Angelina took a feather tickler from a nearby stand, its soft plumes a stark contrast to the dungeon's instruments. She drew teasing patterns on Kai's inner thighs, reveling in his sharp intakes of breath, his muscles tensing under her delicate touch.

"You're so responsive, Kai," Angelina murmured, trailing the feather higher, closer to his impressive manhood. "It excites me to see you so utterly consumed."

Kai, his eyes closed in blissful surrender, relished the sensation of the soft feathers dancing on his skin. "It's a unique feeling, Angelina... light and ticklish, yet it ignites a fire. I can't help but react to your touch."

She continued her teasing exploration, trailing the feathers down his arms, over his sensitive inner elbows, and along his sides, eliciting a symphony of shivers and gasps from him.

"I am utterly at your mercy," Kai confessed, his voice strained with desire, his body trembling.

Smiling, she leaned in, her lips brushing his ear. "You are my love."

Then it was Kai's turn. Angelina, with a playful sigh, allowed him to roll the dice for her. The dice landed on "eyes" and "blindfold." "Ah, delicious," he murmured, his voice a low, seductive rumble. "I choose... to blindfold your eyes, my siren."

Angelina, with a playful sigh, allowed him to tie a crimson blindfold over her eyes. The world plunged into delicious darkness, heightening her other senses. She felt Kai's presence, the warmth of his body, the subtle scent of his skin, now amplified.

From the box, Kai chose a small, cool metal roller, trailing it slowly down her spine, then over her inner thighs, eliciting a gasp. He then rubbed his hardness around her lips. He would pull away when she attempted to lick his stiffness. He rubbed his cock all over her face, titillating her. The heat from his erection triggered instant wetness. Angelina's nectar drizzled down her thighs.

The game continued, each turn bringing them closer to the edge of desire, pushing their boundaries further into the realm of the forbidden. The dungeon, with its intimate setting, amplified the erotic atmosphere.

As the game progressed, the intensity escalated. Angelina, her confidence still buzzing from her dominant role in the grotto, found herself reveling in the vulnerability of being blindfolded, trusting Kai to guide her through new sensations. Kai, in turn, delighted in orchestrating her pleasure, his voice a low, seductive rumble as he described how he would use his tool to create the sensations she was experiencing. His need for control, a key aspect of his personality, was fully engaged.

The soft lighting and the palpable anticipation hanging heavy in the air created an intoxicating ambiance, a world built purely for their shared pleasure.

As the game progressed, Angelina's and Kai's moans became more frequent, their bodies shifting with unrestrained desire. They were fully immersed, their senses heightened, their inhibitions dissolving.

Chapter 6: Boundless Pleasures

Angelina then straddled his face, her position granting him an intimate view of her most secret desires. "Take in my scent, Kai. Breathe me in. Let yourself be consumed by my essence."

Kai did as she instructed, his nose inhaling her intoxicating essence, his tongue teasing her, tasting her, a low moan rumbling in his chest. The vibrations sent a jolt through her core, and she gripped the velvet cushions of the chair, her body beginning to tremble as he worshipped her with his mouth.

His tongue delved deeper, his hands reaching up to hold her hips, pulling her closer, his face buried in her core. Angelina, her breath quickening, struggled to maintain her composure, the sensations becoming too intense, too overwhelming.

Kai's tongue ventured lower, his breath hot against her sensitive skin. He teased her with soft laps, his tongue flicking and swirling, driving her wild. Then, he surprised her by shifting his focus, his tongue finding her most sensitive area – her backdoor.

Angelina gasped, her body tensing as a rush of unexpected pleasure shot through her. "Kai, there... oh, yes, right there," she panted, her body writhing above him, her fingers digging into the chair's armrests.

Kai's tongue worked its magic, circling, probing, driving her closer to the edge. Her body began to shake uncontrollably, her breath coming in short, ragged gasps. "I'm cumming, Kai. Almost there," she warned, her voice tight with anticipation, on the verge of shattering.

With a final, skilled stroke of his tongue, Kai sent her spiraling over the edge. Her orgasm washed over her, intense and all-consuming, a tidal wave of pleasure. Kai continued to lap up her essence, his own body shuddering in response to her powerful release.

Chapter 7: The Shared Canvas of Desire

As Angelina's body slowly settled from the profound climax, Kai's eyes, filled with passion and a triumphant glint, locked onto hers. "I want to touch you, taste you, and return the pleasure tenfold. I want to unleash my own storm." His words held a new depth, reflecting his desire for a deeper intimacy beyond just physical pleasure.

Kai wasted no time. He reached for her, pulling her close, his mouth claiming hers in a hungry kiss that tasted of her own essence. Their tongues danced together, tasting each other, their desire reignited with a furious intensity.

"I want to feel your hands on me, Kai. Everywhere," she whispered, her breath warm on his skin, her body already aching for his touch.

He obliged, his hands roaming her body with a mixture of urgency and reverence. He explored her curves, his touch both firm and gentle, knowing exactly how to drive her wild. His mouth followed suit, placing open-mouthed kisses along her collarbone, down her chest, and over her breasts, suckling and teasing.

Angelina, arching into his touch, threaded her fingers through his hair, holding him close, guiding his mouth. "Your mouth, Kai. It's magic. Pure, unadulterated magic."

He chuckled, the vibrations sending a delightful shiver down her spine. "Then let me work my magic on you, my tempest."

Kai positioned her on the lounge chair, spreading her legs wide, an open invitation to her deepest core. His fingers traced delicate patterns on her inner thighs, teasing her, building the anticipation to an almost unbearable level.

"You're so beautiful, Angelina." he murmured, his breath hot against her core, his eyes devouring her.

Angelina, her head thrown back, moaned, her hands grasping the edges of the chair. "Sì, Kai, lì. Più forte. Più veloce!" (Yes, Kai, right there. Harder. Faster!)

He intensified his efforts, his tongue and fingers working in sync, pushing her closer to the edge, to the precipice of another shattering climax.

In a moment of raw, unbridled passion, Angelina yelled out, "Smack my ass, Kai! Smack it hard!"

Kai paused, his eyes gleaming with a mix of surprise and delight. "Oh, Angelina," he drawled, his voice low and sensual. "That's how you like it? Now, we're truly vibing. I didn't know we could go here together, but I'm thrilled we can." He delivered a sharp, resounding smack to her ass, the sound echoing off the dungeon walls. "You like it rough, don't you? My wild Italian." His dominant nature, usually kept private, was now fully unleashed.

"Sì, Kai, per favore. Più forte," (Yes, Kai, please. Harder,) she urged, her voice thick with desire, her body arching into the sting.

Kai needed no further encouragement. He grabbed her hips, his movements becoming more forceful, their bodies slamming together, the rhythmic thud of flesh against flesh filling the night air, a primal beat accompanying their passionate dance.

Kai's mouth found her ear, his breath hot and heavy. "I want to tie you up, Angelina. Bind you to the bed and have my way with you. Explore every inch of your surrender." This was the core of his BDSM exploration, his need for control and deep intimacy.

At his words, Angelina's core clenched, her desire spiraling higher, her body dripping with anticipation. "Sì, Kai. Incatenami. Rendimi tua. Mostrami tutto." (Yes, Kai. Restrain me. Make me yours. Show me everything.)

Kai's hands tightened on her hips, his thrusts becoming more urgent, more demanding. He painted a vivid picture with his words, describing the bondage scenarios he planned to unleash, the delicious helplessness she would experience. Angelina, caught in a web of anticipation, couldn't help but get wetter, her pleasure intensifying with each filthy promise, each whispered fantasy.

As their pace quickened, Angelina cried out, her body tensing as another powerful orgasm washed over her, a wave of pure bliss. Kai, driven by her response, continues his relentless thrusts, his own pleasure mounting, but held in check by his practiced control, savoring her climax.

Angelina, still riding the waves of her release, pushed Kai onto his back. She straddles him, taking charge once more, her movements fierce and determined. Kai, always up for a challenge, met her vigor with his own, their bodies slamming together in perfect sync, a powerful, primal dance.

The night air was filled with their passionate cries, their sweat-soaked bodies glistening in the moonlight. Their movements became wilder, their passion unrestrained as they drove each other to the brink over and over, exploring every facet of their shared desires.

Finally, spent and sated, they collapsed into each other's arms, their hearts pounding, their breathing labored. They fall asleep in that tangled embrace, their bodies still joined, the candlelight casting a soft glow over their exhausted forms, the scent of sex and salt lingering in the air.

Chapter 8: Kai's Sanctuary of Sensation

Over the next few weeks, Angelina and Kai's adventures continued, each day bringing a new thrill, a deeper exploration of their uninhibited desires. Kai, with his boundless energy and insatiable thirst for excitement, led them to hidden coves, uncharted reefs, and vibrant local celebrations. Their connection deepened with every shared laugh, every daring exploit, and every moment of raw, unbridled passion. He truly was her catalyst, a force that swept away her inhibitions and showed her depths of desire she never knew existed. He taught her to be bold, unapologetic, and utterly free in her sensuality.

One sweltering afternoon, after a particularly exhilarating dive through a labyrinthine coral garden, Kai turned to her, a mischievous glint in his deep ocean eyes. "Angelina," he said, his voice low and conspiratorial. "I have a special night planned. Something to truly surprise you. It involves my place, and a deeper dive into our... shared interests." He paused, a flicker of vulnerability in his gaze. "This is a part of me I don't share with many. It's where I truly let go, where I find a different kind of freedom, a different kind of control."

They arrived at Kai's sprawling beachside villa. Angelina's heart raced as Kai led her down a discreet, spiral staircase to a part of his home she hadn't seen before, felt a thrill of anticipation. It was a stark contrast to her own dungeon. Kai's villa, with its hidden chambers, beckoned her to explore. The air grew heavy with anticipation, and soft, strategically placed lighting cast an intimate, almost theatrical glow over the space. It was a meticulously designed chamber, decadent, a symphony of rich jewel tones – deep emeralds, ruby reds, and sapphire blues –

accented with polished dark wood and gleaming brass. Restraints of various materials – soft silks, supple leather, sturdy ropes – adorned the walls like museum art, alongside an array of whips, chains, ropes, and other sensory delights.

With a sense of pride, Kai explains, "I designed this space to channel my own need for control and deep intimacy. You said you wanted to delve deeper into the world of bondage, and I've prepared a special evening for us." He paused, his gaze softening. "This is a space for letting go, for trust. And trust, Angelina, is powerful." His words emphasized his own journey towards vulnerability. He continued, "My life as a free diver is about pushing limits, but it also requires immense discipline and control. This room is an extension of that, a place where I can explore the boundaries of control, both giving and receiving, in a way that feels deeply personal and freeing."

Angelina's eyes widened as she took in the scene, a gasp escaping her full lips. The main chamber was a vast playground of desires. Kai's collection of toys was on full display, each piece a testament to the history of eroticism. From ancient artifacts to modern creations, they were a testament to the evolution of pleasure. The attendants, dressed provocatively, yet elegant, BDSM attire – leather corsets, sheer stockings, and collars – moved silently, serving them a decadent, sensual dinner. A spread of glistening oysters, plump, chocolate-covered strawberries, and chilled champagne awaited them, along with exotic fruits and delicate pastries, each dish designed to awaken the senses. The very air seemed to spark with erotic possibility, the scent of desire already mingling with the rich aromas of the food. Angelina's eyes widened at the sight. "It's like a museum of ecstasy." Kai's laugh was deep and rich. "Indeed, my curious student. But tonight, these artifacts will come to life."

"Let's enjoy a night of sensual taste, textures and touch." Angelina's senses were heightened as she surrendered to the torrent of sensations Kai orchestrated. His hands, skilled and gentle, guided her through a maze of pleasure, each touch sending shivers down her spine. But it was the unexpected participation of the attendants that added a thrilling twist to their erotic games.

Feathers brushed against Angelina's skin, igniting a trail of goosebumps. Blindfolded, she relied on touch and sound, the soft caress of feathers. The scent of arousal filled the air, mingling with the aroma of chocolate and strawberries, enhancing the multisensory experience.

Kai's whispers guided her, suggesting new tastes and textures to explore. The chill of champagne on her skin, the burst of sweetness from a strawberry, the silky feel of chocolate, melting against her body, each sensation built upon the last, creating a symphony of pleasure.

The attendants' participation added a layer of intrigue. Hands, soft and skilled, joined Kai's, offering a diverse array of touches. Sensations overlapped and intertwined, creating a tapestry of delight that threatened to overwhelm, but Kai's steady presence kept her anchored, eager to explore further.

"Tell me, Angelina, what do you desire now?" Kai's voice, low and commanding, cut through the haze of pleasure.

Angelina, breathless and exhilarated, discovered a newfound confidence. "I want to explore more. The cuffs, the chains...I want to feel their caress, experience the surrender." The thought of surrendering control, something so alien to her business life, was becoming increasingly appealing.

"Then surrender, my student, and let the artifacts of ecstasy do their work."

As Kai unlocks the glass case, a sense of anticipation fills the room. Kai's voice, low and commanding, resonates through the chamber. "Are you ready, Angelina? To explore the intersection of pleasure and pain?" Angelina, her heart racing, nods, her desire clear. "I am, Kai. I trust you to show me the way." The glass case opens with a soft click, revealing an array of tools designed for pleasure and sensation. Kai selects a set of soft cuffs, the leather supple and inviting. He approaches Angelina, his eyes dark with desire.

"These," he says, his voice husky, "will adorn your beautiful wrists. A symbol of your surrender."

Angelina's breath quickens as Kai secures the cuffs around her wrists, the leather a sensual caress against her skin. The attendants assists, gently lifting her arms above her head, securing the cuffs to a sturdy chain. She hangs mid-air, her body on display, vulnerable yet powerful in her surrender.

With deliberate movements, Kai selects a whip, its braided leather falling softly against his arm. "This," they say, "is an instrument of sensation. It can deliver a sting, a bite, or a caress, depending on how it's used." Angelina's eyes widen, anticipation mixing with a hint of nervousness. "And the chains? They seem so stark, so unyielding." A soft smile plays on Kai's lips. "Chains can be both restrictive and liberating. They can hold you captive, but they can also offer a sense of security and surrender. They are a physical manifestation of the power exchange, a way to channel my own need for control."

Angelina's pulse quickens as Kai selects the whip, her curiosity mingling with a hint of trepidation. She has always been intrigued by the interplay of pleasure and pain, and

Kai's guidance promises to lead her on a journey of discovery.

"I've never felt the sting of a whip before," she admits, her voice laced with anticipation. "Will it hurt?"

Kai's eyes hold hers, their gaze intense yet reassuring. "It can, but it's a sensation unlike any other. The sting of the whip is sharp and immediate, a contrast to the caress of the braided leather. It's all about how it's used, and the trust between the giver and receiver."

Angelina nods, her desire evident. "I trust you, Kai. I'm ready."

A soft smile plays on Kai's lips, his confidence reassuring. "I'll guide you through it, angel. We'll start slow, and you can tell me how it affects you."

With gentle movements, Kai runs the whip's braided leather over Angelina's skin, the soft falls tickling her arms and shoulders. The sensation is unique, a mix of texture and subtle bite. Angelina shivers, her breath catching at the new feeling.

"How does it make you feel?" Kai asks, his voice low and intimate.

"It's... intriguing," Angelina replies, her eyes fluttering closed as she focuses on the sensation. "It's like a thousand tiny fingers dancing on my skin."

Kai chuckles, the sound sending a thrill through her. "And now, for the sting."

With a swift movement, Kai delivers a light strike to her shoulder, the whip's fall landing with a soft crack. Angelina's breath catches, a sharp sensation shooting through her, quickly dissipating into a warm glow.

"Incredible," she whispers, her eyes opening wide. "It's like a burst of electricity."

Kai nods, his eyes shining with understanding. "It's a unique sensation, isn't it? Now, for the chains."

Kai reaches for the stark metal links, their coldness a contrast to the warmth of the whip. They drape the chains over Angelina's body, the weight and texture a distinct difference from the softness of the leather. Angelina's desire to understand the chain's purpose and potential deepens. Kai's eyes shine with excitement as they secure the chain around her waist, the links a sensual contrast to her soft skin. "Chains connect us to our desires, Angelina. They bind us to our fantasies, our darkest cravings. Within their embrace, we're free to explore the unknown—our hidden wants and needs."

"How does this make you feel?"

Angelina shivers, the chains sending a different message to her brain. "It's... powerful. I feel vulnerable, but also secure. It's like surrendering to something greater than myself." The thought of applying this kind of surrender and trust, not just in pleasure, but in her business, began to take root.

Kai's eyes soften; his expression filled with affection. "You're doing beautifully, angel. We'll continue to explore, and you'll discover just how liberating these chains can be." "How so, Kai? How can chains offer connection and exploration?" "And how do they ground and center us, Kai?" Kai's hands slide down her arms, his touch sending shivers through her body. "Chains provide structure, stability. They become an anchor, a foundation from which to explore. Within their confines, you're free to let go, to discover new heights of pleasure and sensation."

The clink of the chains sends a thrill through Angelina, the weight of the metal, a tangible reminder of her surrender. The cold links contrast with her warm skin, sending shivers down her arms. Her callused wrists, usually a symbol of her labor, now felt exquisitely vulnerable, yet held securely by the silk, a surprising new sensation. "It's almost like an anchor, grounding me, centering me within the storm of sensations."

Kai's voice is soft, his touch gentle. "Exactly, Angelina. That anchor offers you stability, a foundation from which to explore. It's through surrender that we find freedom." Kai's gaze intensifies, his eyes reflecting the depth of his connection. "Your trust humbles me, Angelina. I promise to respect your boundaries while pushing you to explore new sensations."

Angelina nods, her breath quickening as anticipation builds. "I'm ready for more, Kai. I want to feel the full intensity of the whip."

A soft smile plays on Kai's lips, his confidence reassuring. "As you wish, my beautiful submissive. But first, I want to heighten your senses even further." He blindfolds her again.

The loss of sight intensifies her other senses, the sounds and sensations in the room taking on a new significance.

"Better," Kai murmurs, his breath ghosting over her ear. "Now, you'll feel the whip's caress and sting."

Angelina's heart races as she hears the soft swish of the whip cutting through the air. The anticipation is almost unbearable, her body tingling with excitement. She feels Kai's presence move away, the swish of his feet on the floor indicating distance.

"Are you ready, Angelina?" Kai's voice echoes through the chamber.

"Sì," (Yes,) she breathes, her body taut with expectation.

The first strike lands with a sharp crack, the whip's fall landing just below her bound wrists. Angelina's breath catches, a sharp sting shooting through her arm. It's a unique sensation, intense and immediate.

"Good?" Kai asks, his voice laced with concern.

"Sì," (Yes,) she whispers, her body tingling. "Di più, per favore." (More, please.)

Kai obliges, the next strike landing just below the first. The sting is sharper, more intense, and Angelina bites her lip, her body arching slightly to meet the sensation.

"Again," she pleads, her voice hoarse with need.

Kai delivers another strike, this time on her upper back. The whip's fall lands with a satisfying crack, the sensation sending a jolt through her body. Angelina's head falls back, a soft moan escaping her lips.

"Your skin is so responsive, Angelina," Kai praises, "It sings with each strike."

Angelina smiles, her body on fire. "Then keep playing this song, Maestro."

Kai chuckles, the sound sending vibrations through her body. "As you wish, my beautiful melody."

The whip continues its dance on Angelina's skin, each strike a precise note in their erotic symphony.

Angelina's breath quickens as the attendants, a man and a woman, approach, her body buzzing with anticipation. She feels the gentle weight of the nipple clamps as they secure them in place, a new sensation that sends a thrill through her body. The clamps tighten with each breath, a constant reminder of her arousal.

The woman's lips and tongue trail down Angelina's neck, her touch feather-light and teasing. The man's hands roam her body, caressing her skin with a mixture of gentleness and desire. Their exploration is methodical, their mouths and hands working in sync.

"Mmm, your skin is so soft, Angelina," the woman purrs, her lips brushing Angelina's collarbone. "So responsive to our touch."

Angelina moans, her head falling back as their tongues and lips work magic on her sensitive skin. The clamps tighten with each moan, sending sharp jolts of pleasure through her body. The combination of the blindfold and the clamps heightens her senses, every touch and taste amplified.

Kai's presence looms, his energy filling the space around them. He adjusts the clamps, tightening them just a fraction, and Angelina's breath catches.

"You like that, don't you, angel?" Kai teases, his voice laced with desire. "The pleasure and the pain."

"Sì," (Yes,) she whispers, her body arching slightly. "It's a delicious contrast."

The attendants continue their exploration, their mouths and hands working in harmony.

They lick and suck their way down her body, their tongues leaving trails of fire in their wake. The clamps tighten with each new sensation, intensifying her arousal.

"Oh, there's so much more to explore," the man murmurs, his lips brushing her stomach. "So many ways to pleasure you."

Angelina can only moan in response, her body alive with sensation. The clamps bite into her nipples, the pleasure and pain merging into a heady mix that clouds her mind. Kai's touch is a constant, his hands guiding the attendants, his breath hot on her skin.

"You're doing beautifully, angel," Kai praises, his fingers gently brushing her hair back. "Surrender to the sensations. Let go."

Angelina nods, her body trembling on the edge of release. The attendants work in sync, their mouths and hands moving lower, their tongues teasing her most sensitive areas.

The clamps tighten further, sending sharp spikes of pleasure through her core.

"Kai," she breathes, her body on the brink. "Sono quasi lì." (I'm—almost there.)

Kai's voice is a low rumble, his desire evident. "Come for us, Angelina. Let go."

Angelina's release hits her like a wave, her body shaking as pleasure washes over her. The clamps tighten further, intensifying her climax, her cries echoing through the chamber. As Angelina comes down from her high, she feels Kai's embrace from behind, his arms wrapping around her, his body warm against hers. She can feel his arousal pressing against her, a reminder of his own desire.

His hands cup her breasts gently, his thumbs brushing her sensitive nipples. The sensation sends a jolt through her, her body still buzzing from her intense release. Kai rocks her slowly, his hips moving in a gentle rhythm that has her biting her lip.

"You did so well, angel," he murmurs, his lips brushing her ear. "So responsive, so beautiful."

Angelina leans back into his embrace, her eyes closing as she relishes the afterglow of her climax. Kai's touch is gentle, his hands roaming her body with tender possession. The attendants work efficiently, removing the leg restraints, freeing her movements.

"Thank you," she whispers, her voice hoarse from her cries. "That was... incredible."

Kai chuckles, his breath tickling her ear. "I'm glad you enjoyed it. But we're not done yet, my beautiful submissive."

Angelina smiles, her body still humming with pleasure. "I'm yours to command, Kai."

Angelina's exploration of tastes, textures, and sensations is guided by Kai's expertise and the attendants' participation, adding layers of pleasure and depth to the experience. The inclusion of cuffs and chains introduces the concept of restraint and surrender, highlighting the importance of trust and boundaries within BDSM dynamics.

As the games progressed, Angelina surrendered fully to the experience. Her body was a canvas, and Kai and his attendants were the artists, painting with feathers, chocolate, and champagne. The scent of arousal hung heavy in the air, a testament to the pleasure they were creating.

The room buzzes with erotic energy as couples intertwine their passion on full display. Angelina's breath quickens as she takes in the sight, her inhibitions melting away. She feels exposed, her desire hanging heavy in the air, but the exhibitionist side of her relishes the moment.

Kai's gaze never leaves her, and she knows he's watching her take in the pleasure around them. Her nipples pebble, betraying her arousal. With a naughty smile, she spreads her legs slightly, a silent invitation for Kai to join her. Some of the attendants watch as Kai gracefully begins to devour Angelina in front of them. They watch with intense focus. Angelina loves the attention. There are also a few of the attendants off in the distance in a full uproar of pleasure. Angelina cannot take her eyes off them fucking.

Kai drops to his knees before her. His erection strains against his pants, but his focus is on pleasing Angelina. He captures a nipple between his lips, sucking gently as he teases it with his tongue.

Angelina's head falls back, a soft moan escaping her lips. Kai's mouth on her breast, his warm breath ghosting over sensitive skin, sends sparks of pleasure through her body. She continues to watch the orgy, her eyes taking in the passionate displays even as Kai's mouth works magic on her nipples.

His hands roam over her thighs, caressing and teasing, inching closer to the core of her desire. Angelina's breath quickens as she feels his fingertips graze her inner thighs, his touch feather-light and tantalizing.

"You like watching, don't you, Angelina?" Kai murmurs against her skin, his voice thick with desire.

"Mmm, yes," she whispers, her eyes flitting between the orgy and Kai's head bent over her breast. "It's so erotic, all this pleasure, all these beautiful bodies." The thought sparked something new in her, a daring idea about how to fight her competitor, not with secrecy, but with bold, beautiful display.

Kai chuckles, the vibration against her sensitive nipple making her squirm. "And what else do you like, Angelina? Tell me what you want."

His fingers brush against her core, and she gasps, her hips bucking slightly. "Toccami, Kai," (Touch me, Kai,) she pleads, her eyes closing as she focuses on the sensations he's creating. "Per favore, con le tue mani, la tua bocca..." (Please, with your hands, your mouth...)

Kai obliges, his fingers dipping lower, stroking her wetness as his mouth leaves her nipples. He captures her lips in a passionate kiss, his tongue tangling with hers as he tastes her arousal. Then, breaking the kiss, he makes his way lower, his breath hot against her skin.

Angelina's eyes flutter open as Kai settles between her thighs. His gaze, intense and full of promise, holds hers as he begins to pleasure her with his mouth, his skilled tongue sending her spiraling into a vortex of pleasure...

The attendants, ever attentive, refilled their champagne flutes, the bubbles a perfect complement to the electric atmosphere. The soft lighting, the erotic attire of the attendants, and the palpable anticipation hanging heavy in the air created an intoxicating ambiance, a world built purely for their shared pleasure.

Chapter 9: The Orgy and the Voyeur

Eventually, the group's passion consumed them entirely, and the attendants, lost in their own uninhibited pleasure, began to pair off, forming smaller, intensely focused groups. The pleasure chamber became a vibrant tableau of intertwined bodies, a symphony of moans and gasps. It was a truly sexy vibe, raw and unadulterated.

Angelina and Kai, now largely unnoticed, exchanged a look of shared amusement. They chuckled, their movements slow and deliberate, savoring the lingering sensations. They simply lay back on their plush cushions, champagne flutes in hand, and watched.

Angelina was a natural voyeur. It turned her on immensely to watch other people's intimate acts, to witness their uninhibited pleasure. Her gaze was intense, her nipples hard, and her body dripped with sensual intensity as she took it all in, a silent participant in the unfolding drama. This voyeurism, she realized, wasn't just about arousal; it was a deep fascination with the raw, unfiltered expression of human desire, a mirror to her own burgeoning uninhibited self. Kai, watching Angelina's reaction, became harder the more he stared at her, her arousal mirroring his own. He could feel her gaze, and she could feel his, their shared voyeurism igniting a new, potent spark between them. The idea of *being seen*, even indirectly, was thrilling. It made her consider the very public nature of her olive oil brand — how she usually guarded its image so carefully, almost secretly. What if she approached it with the same uninhibited joy she found here?

Kai took her hand, his voice a low rumble. "I want you," he murmured, his thumb stroking her palm. "Let me take you someplace more private." His words, though simple, carried the weight of his desire for deep intimacy.

Chapter 10: The Master's Playroom — Unfettered Desires

Angelina's heart raced as she stepped into Kai's inner sanctum, a private room reserved for his most intimate pleasures. The space was a testament to luxury and sensuality, with soft furs and silks creating an inviting atmosphere. The scent of exotic spices hung heavy in the air, teasing her senses.

At far end of the room stood an original Louis XIV bed, its drapes tied back to reveal inviting silk sheets and an abundance of plush pillows. The bed seemed to beckon to them, promising a night of untold delights.

"Kai, this is..." Angelina trailed off, at a loss for words.

"Magical?" Kai supplied, his eyes sparkling with mischief. "Sensual? The perfect setting for what I have planned." His words hinted at his dominant nature, his desire to orchestrate her pleasure.

Angelina's breath quickened as she imagined the pleasures that awaited her. She reached out, trailing her fingers over the soft silk sheets. "It's fit for royalty."

"And you, my dear, are my queen for the night," Kai purred, stepping closer. "I intend to treat you as such."

He took her hand, leading her towards the bed. With each step, anticipation built, her pulse thrumming in her veins. Kai's eyes never left hers, his gaze intense and full of promise.

"Lie back and let me show you what a night in my inner sanctum entails," he instructed, his voice a sensual lure, a subtle command.

Angelina did as he asked, her body tingling with excitement. She settled onto the bed, the silk sheets caressing her skin. Kai joined her, his body close, his breath warm on her neck.

"Close your eyes, Angelina," he whispered, his fingers gently brushing her eyelids. "Let your senses guide you."

She obeyed, her other senses heightening as her vision was obscured. She felt Kai's lips brush her neck, his hands beginning a slow exploration of her body. The scent of spices filled her lungs, mingling with the heady aroma of their desire.

Soft music began to play, a sultry melody that danced over her skin. Kai's touch was feather-light, his lips and tongue leaving a trail of fire in their wake. Angelina sighed, her body melting into the bed as Kai's skilled hands roamed, igniting a blaze of pleasure...

The silk restraints send a thrill through Angelina, the softness of the fabric contrasting with the strength that holds her wrists captive. She feels exposed and vulnerable, yet incredibly aroused by the loss of control. Kai's every move is a tantalizing promise of what's to come, a clear expression of his dominant nature.

Her eyes widen as Kai reveals the ornate glass dildo, its length impressive and slightly intimidating. She bites her lip, a mix of nerves and excitement fluttering in her stomach. The dildo is a work of art, swirling colors shimmering in the soft light.

"It's beautiful," she breathes, her eyes never leaving the glass shaft.

"I'm glad you appreciate it, Angelina," Kai says, his voice laced with desire. "But it's even more stunning when it's inside you."

Her core clenches at his words, anticipation coursing through her veins. Kai takes his time, warming the glass dildo between his hands before teasing her folds with the smooth tip. The warmth is a pleasant contrast to the cool silk of the restraints.

"You're already so wet for me," he murmurs, his breath hot against her ear. "Imagine how good this will feel sliding inside."

Angelina's breath quickens as Kai teases her entrance, the smooth glass providing a unique sensation. He takes his time, letting her adjust to the size, slowly inching the dildo inside. Her body stretches to accommodate the width, a delicious burn that only fuels her desire.

"Oh, Kai," she moans, her head falling back. "Si sente così bene." (It feels so good.)

With gentle but firm strokes, Kai begins to thrust the dildo in and out, finding a rhythm that has Angelina squirming in pleasure. The glass shaft glides smoothly, providing a full sensation that has her biting her lip to muffle her moans.

"Look at you, taking it all," Kai teases, his voice full of admiration. "You're stunning like this, so receptive to my touch."

Angelina's cheeks flush with pleasure, her body on fire. The silk restraints add to the eroticism, restricting her movements, intensifying the sensations coursing through her. Kai leans in, capturing her lips in a passionate kiss as he continues to thrust the dildo deep inside her.

Her hands strain against the silk restraints, her body arching to meet each thrust. The combination of the soft silk and hard glass sends her senses into overdrive, pleasure building with each stroke...

The addition of a vibrating bullet sends Angelina spiraling into a vortex of pleasure. The soft buzz against her sensitive clit is a contrast to the smooth thrusts of the glass dildo. Her body trembles, her breath coming in short gasps as Kai teases her with the new sensation.

"Kai," she moans, her head falling back. "That's—oh, right there."

Kai chuckles, his voice thick with desire. "You like that, do you?"

"Sì," she whispers, her eyes fluttering closed as she focuses on the intense sensations coursing through her body. "Non fermarti, per favore." (Don't stop, please.)

Kai obliges, his thrusts finding a steady rhythm that has the bullet vibrating against her clit with each stroke. The combination of the smooth glass and the relentless vibrations sends shocks of pleasure through her core, her hips bucking involuntarily.

"You're so beautiful like this, Angelina," Kai murmurs, his breath hot against her ear. "So responsive to my touch."

Angelina can only moan in response, her body on fire. Kai's skilled hands roam her body, teasing her nipples, her thighs, adding to the overload of sensations. The silk restraints hold her captive, intensifying the pleasure by restricting her movements.

"I can feel your body trembling," Kai says, his lips brushing her neck. "You're ready to come, aren't you?"

"Sì," she breathes, her voice hoarse with need. "Kai, per favore, non fermarti." (Kai, please, don't stop.)

Kai chuckles, his fingers tightening on the dildo as he increases the speed of his thrusts. The bullet vibrates relentlessly against her clit, sending her hurtling towards the edge. Her back arches, her body straining against the restraints as she surrenders to the pleasure.

"Come for me, Angelina," Kai urges, his voice a sensual command. "Let go."

Angelina's release hits her like a wave, crashing over her and sweeping her away. Her moans fill the room as her body shakes with the force of her climax. Kai continues his relentless thrusts, milking every last drop of ecstasy from her trembling body.

As her release ebbs, Kai slows his movements, a satisfied smile on his lips. He removes the dildo and vibrating bullet, leaving her body humming with satisfaction. He releases her wrists from the silk restraints, gently caressing her sensitive skin.

Angelina's eyes flutter open, her body boneless and satisfied. She reaches for Kai, pulling him close for a passionate kiss, tasting herself on his lips.

"That was..." she begins, her voice trailing off as she searches for the right words.

"Incredible," Kai supplies, his eyes sparkling with satisfaction. "I'm glad you enjoyed it, my beautiful Angelina."

Angelina smiles, snuggling into his embrace. "Enjoyed it? I think 'life-altering' is more accurate." The idea of *letting go* and *trusting* someone else with such profound vulnerability felt like a direct counterpoint to her solitary battle for the farm.

Kai chuckles, his arms tightening around her. "Well, we're not done yet. There's much more pleasure to be had."

Chapter 11: The Art of Control and Submission

Angelina's eyes sparkle at the promise in his words. "I can't wait."

The scent of exotic flowers fills the air as Kai guides Angelina into an oversized bathtub. The warm water and soft bubbles envelope her, the scent relaxing her mind and body. Kai's attendant, dressed in a tight latex French maid's outfit, adds to the eroticism of the moment.

Angelina leans back, her eyes closing as the attendant gently lathers her body with a soft sponge. The attendant's touch is both respectful and sensual, sending shivers down Angelina's spine. She can feel Kai's eyes on her, his gaze intense as he takes in the scene before him. His need for control was evident, even in this silent moment.

As the attendant rinses the soap from Angelina's body, she stands up, the water cascading down her skin. She turns to the attendant, her desire evident in her eyes. Without a word, she pulls the attendant close, capturing her lips in a passionate kiss.

The attendant melts into the kiss, their lips moving in perfect sync. Angelina's hands roam over the smooth latex, her fingers finding the zipper at the back. She pulls it down, exposing the attendant's bare skin.

Angelina breaks the kiss, her eyes filled with desire. She pulls the attendant's latex panties down, baring her most intimate area. Without hesitation, Angelina sinks to her knees, her mouth finding the attendant's center.

Kai's breath catches as he watches the scene unfold. He had expected to bathe with Angelina, but this unexpected turn of events has him enthralled. He steps into the bathtub and sits down, his eyes never leaving the two women. His hand moves to his erection, stroking himself as he watches Angelina pleasure the attendant with abandon. This was a different facet of his BDSM exploration, witnessing her take control.

The attendant moans, her hands tangling in Angelina's hair as she returns the oral favor. Their tongues dance, their passion on full display. Angelina's fingers delve deeper, their wet sounds filling the room.

Kai's strokes become more urgent as he watches the women lose themselves in each other. Their moans and whispers echo off the tiles, creating a sensual symphony. The attendant's wet body shines in the soft light, contrasting with Angelina's naked form.

Angelina's skilled tongue brings the attendant to the edge, her body trembling as they climax. Kai's breath quickens as he watches, his own release building. The attendant's cries of pleasure fill the room, her body arching into Angelina's mouth.

As the attendant comes down from her high, Angelina stands, her body glistening with water and arousal. She pulls Kai close, kissing him deeply, tasting herself on his lips. He responds eagerly, his hands roaming her body as their kisses grow more frantic.

The attendant, still buzzing from her own release, joins in, caressing Angelina's body, her lips seeking Kai's. The three of them tangle together, their passion and desire fueling an intense erotic scene.

Kai's pleasure is evident as Angelina and the attendant work in harmony to pleasure him. Their mouths and hands move in sync, exploring his body with devotion. He leans back, his hands behind his head, surrendering to their touch.

"You two are incredible," he breathes, his eyes closed in bliss. "The best dessert I could ask for."

Angelina smiles, her hands trailing down his chest. "We aim to please, my love."

The attendant nods, her lips brushing Kai's neck. "And there's more to come, if you're up for it."

Kai's eyes flash open, his desire clear. "Oh, I'm definitely up for it."

Angelina chuckles, her fingers trailing lower. "Good. Because I have plans for you, sir."

With that, she takes charge, positioning herself above Kai's face. The attendant moves in sync, straddling Kai's hips. Their moans mingle as Angelina lowers herself onto his mouth, his tongue immediately seeking her core.

Kai's hands grasp Angelina's hips, holding her in place as he feasts on her sweetness. The attendant begins to ride Kai's cock, her pace matching the rhythm of his tongue. Their kisses and caresses are fervent, their nipples brushing, their breath intermingling.

"Oh, yes, just like that," Kai groans, his hips thrusting upward to meet the attendant's downward motion.

Angelina's head falls back, her body trembling as Kai's tongue works its magic. The attendant's hands roam Angelina's body, her kisses and touches creating a symphony of pleasure. Their moans echo off the walls, their passion fueling the intensity of their movements.

As Kai's tongue brings Angelina to the edge, the attendant's pace quickens, her breath coming in short gasps. Angelina's thighs clench around Kai's face, her body tensing as her release builds. The attendant's hands tighten on Angelina's hips, her own climax approaching.

"Come for me, both of you," Kai urges, his tongue flicking relentlessly.

Angelina cries out, her body shaking as her release washes over her. The attendant follows suit, her body stiffening as they climax, her cries mingling with Angelina's. Kai's mouth is filled with her essence, his cock spent and satisfied.

The attendant, dismounts from Kai's ejaculating rod, leans down, sucking the release of his semen from his cock into her mouth. Kai groans, his body tingling with the aftershocks of his release. He thanks the attendant with a kiss, his hands caressing her body.

Wrapping Angelina in a soft towel, Kai leads her to his personal bedroom. They spend the night entwined, their touches gentle and loving. Kai's fingers trace patterns on Angelina's skin, his lips brushing soft kisses along her shoulder. Their murmurs and caresses continue through the night, until eventually, they drift into a peaceful slumber.

Chapter 12: The Playful Adventure

The following morning, Angelina awoke in Kai's arms, the lingering scent of sex and leather still clinging to their skin.

"Good morning, my wild one," Kai murmured, his lips brushing her forehead. "Ready for more adventures?"

Angelina stretched, her muscles pleasantly sore. "Always. What delights do you have planned for today?" She glanced at her phone, seeing a few missed calls from her farm manager, Marco. The familiar anxiety twinged, but this time, instead of pushing it away, she felt a flicker of something new: confidence. *Later*, she thought. *Today, I embrace this, and then I'll address that with a new kind of power.*

Kai grinned. "Today, we take our play outside. The ocean calls, and with it, new opportunities for... exploration." He sat up, pulling her gently with him. "But first, tell me about your olive oil. What makes it so special? I grew up on various coastlines, moving with my marine biologist parents, so I've seen a lot of different lands. Yours sounds unique." His genuine interest, a crack in his emotionally guarded exterior, was a subtle sign of his deepening connection. He continued, "My parents were always chasing the perfect research site, from the Great Barrier Reef to the icy waters of the Arctic. I learned early on that freedom meant adapting, exploring, and sometimes, letting go of what you thought you knew. That's why I became a free diver – it's all about control, yes, but also about trusting your body, and the ocean itself."

Angelina, surprised by the genuine interest in his voice, found herself talking about the Tuscan sun, the ancient trees, the meticulous pressing process, the pride in her family's legacy. She spoke of the competitor, a shadow she usually kept hidden, and the frustration of feeling constantly on the defensive. Kai listened intently, asking thoughtful questions. "It sounds like you pour your soul into it," he commented. "That's why it's world-renowned. It's not just oil, it's a story, a passion. Just like free diving for me. It's not just holding your breath, it's a connection. And sometimes, the best way to hold your breath is to trust the current, not fight it." His understanding touched something deep within her, a connection beyond the physical, hinting at his own journey of learning to trust and be vulnerable.

Later that afternoon, while lounging by the pool, Angelina picked up her phone again. She saw another email from Marco, highlighting a new challenge from the competitor. But instead of the usual dread, a new resolve settled over her. She thought of Kai's words about trust, about surrendering to the current. She thought of her own experiences in his pleasure palace, trusting him with her most vulnerable self. Her anxieties, though still present, felt less overwhelming, now tempered by a growing sense of empowerment.

She opened her phone and called Marco. His voice, usually deferential, sounded strained. "Signora Rossi, the new competitor, they're... very aggressive. They've undercut our price by 15% with 'La Forza', a new mass-produced blend, and they're targeting our key distributors in Milan and Rome. I've tried to negotiate, but they're relentless. I don't know what to do about this latest move."

Angelina took a deep breath. "Marco," she said, her voice calm and steady, surprising even herself. "I'm calling you because I trust you. You've been with the farm since my father's time. You know the land, you know our process, you know our people. I've been trying to control everything from afar, but I realize now that's not the answer. I need you to take the lead. You have my full authority. Make the decisions you think are best for the farm. I'm here for consultation, but I'm putting my faith in your hands. We will fight this, but we will fight it together, and with our own unique strengths."

There was a stunned silence on the other end of the line. "Signora? Are you... are you serious?" Marco's hesitation stemmed from years of working under her father's strict, centralized control, and then Angelina's initial attempts to replicate that. He had always had ideas, but no real power to implement them.

"Completely serious, Marco. I trust you. Show them what you can do. *Fidati di te stesso.*" (Trust yourself.)

Marco, initially shocked, found a newfound empowerment in Angelina's words. He spent the next few weeks working tirelessly, implementing bold new strategies he'd always wanted to try but never dared to suggest. He leveraged his local connections, securing exclusive deals with smaller, high-end trattorias in Tuscany that valued authenticity over price. He initiated a grassroots marketing campaign, organizing olive oil tasting events in local markets, highlighting the superior quality and artisanal process of their *Olio della Novella* compared to the mass-produced competitor. He even started a social media campaign, showcasing the beauty of their Tuscan groves and the dedication of their workers, connecting consumers directly to the source. The results were not immediate, but there was a palpable shift in the farm's momentum. Marco sent Angelina regular, excited updates, filled with a zealous energy she hadn't heard from him in years.

Angelina's days with Kai became a blur of exhilarating activities, each one seamlessly blending into an opportunity for erotic indulgence. Kai, a professional free diver and ocean exploration guide, introduced Angelina to the thrill of underwater photography. He taught her how to hold her breath, how to move gracefully through the water, and how to capture the vibrant marine life. He spoke of setting regional records as a teenager, of the obsession with pushing limits, a drive Angelina recognized within herself. He also shared stories of the financial realities of his nomadic lifestyle, how he secured sponsorships from high-end diving gear companies and organized exclusive, high-paying expeditions for wealthy thrill-seekers, balancing his passion with the practicalities of earning a living.

One afternoon, they were exploring a newly discovered coral reef, its colors a kaleidoscope of blues, greens, and purples. Angelina, wearing only a sheer, barely-there swimsuit, was focused on framing a shot of a school of iridescent fish. Kai, swimming just behind her, his powerful body a silent shadow, reached out and gently pulled her against him.

His hands roamed her waist, then slid under the thin fabric of her suit, cupping her bare buttocks. He pressed his hard erection against her, the sensation electrifying in the cool water. Angelina gasped, her breath escaping in a stream of bubbles.

"Lost in your art, my love?" he whispered against her ear, his voice muffled by the water. "Or lost in me?"

She giggled, a playful sound that vibrated through the water. "Both, Kai. Always both."

He began to thrust gently, slowly, his movements in sync with the gentle current. Angelina leaned back into him, her body molding against his, the friction of their wet skin against the thin fabric of her suit sending shivers of pleasure through her. The fish, oblivious, continued to dart around them, as if they were just another part of the vibrant ecosystem.

Kai then pulled her into a small, secluded underwater cave, barely large enough for their bodies. The light filtered in from above, creating an ethereal glow. He pressed her against the cool, smooth rock, his mouth finding hers in a deep, hungry kiss. Their tongues tangled, tasting of salt and passion.

He stripped her swimsuit off with a swift movement, then shed his own. Their naked bodies, buoyant in the water, moved together, Kai entering her with a powerful thrust. Angelina cried out, the sound muffled by the water, her hands grasping the rough rock for support.

They made love in the underwater cave, their movements slow and deliberate, the water providing a unique resistance. The pleasure was intense, amplified by the secrecy and the raw, primal setting. Angelina felt utterly consumed, her body a vessel for his pleasure, her mind lost in the depths of their shared passion. As they surfaced, Kai held her close. "That was for us," he murmured. "A secret, just like the strength you'll find when you face your challenges back home. You don't always have to fight on the surface." Angelina thought of Marco, of the burden she had lifted from her own shoulders by trusting him. The feeling of shared responsibility, even for her business, felt surprisingly light.

Chapter 13: Island Legends and Hidden Desires

Kai, with his deep knowledge of the Bahamian islands and a history of exploring uncharted underwater territories, was a treasure trove of local legends and hidden spots. One evening, over a dinner of freshly caught lobster and chilled white wine, he recounted a tale of a sunken pirate ship, rumored to hold not just gold, but a collection of ancient, erotic artifacts, hidden in a secret grotto accessible only at low tide.

"They say the artifacts are cursed," Kai said, his eyes gleaming mischievously, "to inflame the desires of anyone who touches them." He leaned back, observing her. "But I think the true curse is for those who deny their desires, Angelina. Those who live by other people's rules. My nomadic lifestyle has shown me that. Freedom isn't just about avoiding commitments; it's about embracing who you truly are. And the deepest adventures aren't always solo journeys." Angelina thought of her rigid marketing strategies, the cautious, almost secretive way she had always presented her brand. "Denying desires..." The phrase resonated, a growing conviction that she didn't have to live by those rules anymore, not in her personal life, nor in her business.

Angelina's eyes widened. "A treasure hunt? And a cursed one at that? You know I can't resist a challenge, especially one that promises such... interesting side effects." Her adventurous spirit was fully engaged. She thought of her farm, the conservative expectations of her village. *Denying desires...*

The next morning, armed with maps, diving gear, and a healthy dose of anticipation, they set out. Kai, with his expert navigation honed from years of professional expeditions, guided them through treacherous currents and hidden reefs. After hours of searching, just as the tide began to recede, they found it – a narrow, almost invisible opening in a cliff face, leading into a dark, watery cavern.

They swam into the grotto, the air thick with the scent of salt and damp rock. The light was dim, filtering in from cracks above, casting eerie shadows. And there, nestled among barnacle-covered chests, were the artifacts – not gold, but beautifully carved statues of intertwined lovers, ancient erotic pottery, and scrolls depicting scenes of uninhibited pleasure.

"The curse seems to be working already," Angelina whispered, her voice husky, as she gazed at a particularly explicit statue, her body already tingling. Her sensual nature, always keen, responded immediately.

Kai chuckled, his hand finding her waist, pulling her close. "Indeed. It seems the pirates had excellent taste, both in treasure and in pleasure." He traced the intricate carvings on a ceramic piece. "These people, they embraced life fully. They didn't hide their passions. They understood true freedom." His words echoed his own character arc, the journey from emotional guardedness to vulnerability.

They spent hours in the grotto, not just admiring the artifacts, but becoming part of the art themselves. Surrounded by centuries of unbridled passion, they shed their diving suits, their naked bodies mirroring the poses of the ancient statues. They made love against the cool, damp rock, their moans echoing in the cavern, their passion as timeless as the artifacts around them. Angelina, feeling the weight of history and desire, urged Kai to take her in every position depicted on the scrolls, their bodies becoming a living tableau of ancient lust.

"This is more than treasure, Kai," Angelina panted, her body slick with sweat and desire. "This is a connection to something primal, something eternal." She looked at him, her eyes shining with new understanding. "It makes me wonder what other 'curses' I've been avoiding. What other aspects of myself I've kept hidden. Perhaps even how I run my farm. All that secrecy... it's just another kind of chain."

As they emerged from the grotto, the sun was setting, painting the sky in fiery hues. They were exhausted, but exhilarated, their bodies humming with a new kind of energy. They had found not just a treasure, but a deeper understanding of their own boundless desires, and for Angelina, a growing conviction that this newfound freedom could extend beyond the bedroom, into every corner of her life. She even considered how a bolder approach might help Marco back home.

Chapter 14: The Exhibitionist's Canvas

Their adventures in the Bahamas continued to push the boundaries of their pleasure, blurring the lines between private intimacy and public display. Kai, with his innate theatricality, and Angelina, with her newfound confidence in her own sensuality, found themselves increasingly drawn to the thrill of exhibitionism. It wasn't about shocking or offending, but about the delicious frisson of being seen, of sharing their uninhibited joy with the world, however subtly. This freedom, Angelina realized, felt like a powerful counterpoint to the rigid expectations she faced back in Tuscany, especially concerning her business. *Why hide the beauty of what we create?* she wondered.

One bustling afternoon, they found themselves at a vibrant local market, a kaleidoscope of colors, sounds, and scents. The air was thick with the aroma of grilled conch, sweet plantains, and the rhythmic beat of Junkanoo music drifting from a nearby stall. Angelina wore a flowing, sheer sarong over a tiny bikini, hinting at the curves beneath. Kai was in loose linen shorts, his muscular chest bare. As they browsed stalls overflowing with exotic fruits and handmade crafts, their hands were never far apart.

"Let's play a game, my love," Angelina whispered, her fingers tracing the line of his jaw. "A silent challenge." Her expressive face held a mischievous glint.

Kai's eyes sparkling. "I'm listening."

"We'll see who can get the other to climax, without anyone noticing," she purred, her voice barely audible above the market chatter. "Using only subtle touches, stolen glances, and the power of suggestion." The thought of this hidden display, a secret shared only between them, sparked an idea. *What if I could make my olive oil brand a public display of passion, too?*

Kai's grin was devilish. "Consider it accepted."

They began their game. As they haggled over a carved wooden mask, Angelina's foot brushed against Kai's inner thigh, then slowly, deliberately, began to stroke his impressive cock through his linen shorts. Kai's eyes widened, a barely perceptible gasp escaping him as he tried to maintain a casual demeanor while discussing the price of a seashell necklace.

Then it was his turn. As Angelina admired a vibrant painting, Kai's hand slipped under her sarong, his fingers finding her wetness, teasing her clitoris with feather-light strokes. Angelina bit her lip, a faint flush rising on her olive-toned skin, as she feigned intense interest in the brushstrokes, her hips subtly grinding against his hand.

The market became their stage, the unsuspecting crowds their audience. They exchanged suggestive glances, their eyes burning with shared desire. Angelina would brush past him, her breast grazing his arm, sending shivers through him. Kai would lean in to whisper a comment about a piece of jewelry, his breath hot against her ear, his fingers subtly pinching her nipple through her bikini top.

The tension built, a delicious, unspoken battle of wills. Angelina found herself moaning softly behind a large straw hat as Kai's fingers worked magic between her legs, while Kai nearly dropped a bag of mangoes when Angelina's hand, seemingly innocently, cupped his ass and squeezed.

Finally, as they stood by a bustling fruit stall, Angelina's foot, with a final, exquisite pressure, sent Kai over the edge. He stiffened, a silent groan escaping him, his eyes closing for a fraction of a second before he opened them again, a triumphant, yet discreet, smirk on his face.

"Mangoes are delicious today," he managed, his voice a little strained.

Angelina winked. "Indeed. And quite satisfying." The thrill of this public intimacy, of the hidden pleasure, filled her with a bold inspiration. *My olive oil isn't just a product; it's a passion, a lifestyle. Why am I trying to keep that a secret?*

Later that evening, at a lively beach bar, they continued their game. The air throbbed with the reggae beat, and the scent of grilled fish mingled with salt and sweat. Under the cover of a dimly lit table, Angelina openly stroked Kai's cock through his shorts, her eyes locked with his, daring him to react. He, in turn, slipped his hand under her sundress, fingering her wetness, then pulling her onto his lap, her legs wrapped around him, their bodies grinding together under the table, hidden by the tablecloth, yet in plain sight. The thrill of nearly being caught, the shared secret, amplified their pleasure exponentially.

"This is madness," Angelina whispered, her breath hot against his ear as she felt him swell against her.

"Delicious madness," Kai corrected, his eyes gleaming with uninhibited joy. "The world is our playground, my love. And you, Angelina, are becoming its most fearless player. It's a different kind of freedom than just being solo." Angelina, buzzing with the thrill of exhibitionism, found herself thinking of her farm. A daring idea began to form: a sensual marketing campaign, showcasing the passion and "good life" embodied by her olive oil, rather than just its quality. Something that would make her conservative competitors blush.

Chapter 15: The Sunken Siren's Song

Kai's passion for the ocean was infectious, and Angelina found herself drawn deeper into his world of free diving and underwater exploration. He spoke of a legendary "Sunken Siren," a beautiful, ancient statue rumored to lie in the deepest part of a treacherous coral labyrinth, guarded by strong currents and elusive marine life. It was a dive only the most skilled attempted, and Kai, with his history of setting regional records and leading exclusive expeditions, was determined to find it.

"They say the Siren sings," Kai explained one morning, tracing a complex route on a nautical map. "A song that calls to the deepest desires of those who hear it, leading them to ecstasy or madness." He looked at her, his expression serious, a hint of his own journey towards vulnerability. "But it can also lead to clarity, Angelina. To seeing what you truly want, beyond what you're told you should want. Sometimes, the deepest adventure isn't solo. It's about who you share it with." He paused, a knowing look in his eyes. "Like that farm of yours. Are you still trying to fight that battle alone, or are you letting Marco truly lead?"

Angelina's eyes gleamed. "Madness sounds intriguing. Lead the way, my fearless diver." She thought of the competitor, the endless emails about market share. Clarity sounded like a welcome relief. The idea of a shared adventure, rather than a solo fight, felt increasingly appealing, especially now that she had truly empowered Marco.

The journey to the Siren's resting place was an adventure in itself. They navigated through narrow channels, battled strong underwater currents, and explored vibrant, untouched coral gardens teeming with exotic fish. Kai taught Angelina advanced free-diving techniques, pushing her limits, and she responded with a fierce determination that matched his own. A sudden, swift barracuda darted past, its sharp teeth a stark reminder of the ocean's dangers, adding a thrilling edge to their quest.

Finally, after hours of exhilarating diving, they found it. Nestled in a deep, sapphire-blue cavern, bathed in ethereal light filtering from above, stood the Sunken Siren. She was a breathtaking statue, carved from white marble, her form exquisitely sensual, her face serene, her arms outstretched as if beckoning them closer. The water around her seemed to shimmer with an unseen energy.

As they swam closer, Angelina felt a strange pull, a tingling sensation that started in her core and spread through her limbs. She imagined the Siren's song, a silent melody of pure, unadulterated desire. But within that melody, she also heard a whisper of resolve, a quiet strength settling in.

Kai, his eyes wide with awe, reached for her hand. "She's magnificent," he breathed, his voice muffled by the water.

Angelina nodded, unable to speak, her gaze fixed on the Siren. She felt an overwhelming urge to touch the statue, to absorb its ancient power. As her fingers brushed the cold marble, a jolt, like an electric current, shot through her. It wasn't just sexual; it was a jolt of clarity, a sense of purpose. A renewed conviction that her vision for the farm, the bold, sensual marketing campaign she was now envisioning, was the right path.

Without a word, they shed their diving gear, letting it drift to the sandy bottom. Their naked bodies, illuminated by the otherworldly light, moved towards the Siren. Kai pressed Angelina against the statue's cool, smooth form, his mouth finding hers in a deep, hungry kiss.

They made love against the Sunken Siren, their bodies slick with saltwater, their moans echoing in the cavern, amplified by the water. Angelina wrapped her legs around Kai's waist, her hips grinding against the cold marble, the sensation both jarring and intensely arousing. Kai thrust into her with primal force, his hands gripping the Siren's waist, as if claiming her power for their own.

"She sings to us, Kai," Angelina panted, her voice a raw whisper against his lips. "Il canto del puro desiderio. E di... forza. Di sapere per cosa lottare. E con chi lottare." (The song of pure desire. And of... strength. Of knowing what to fight for. And who to fight with.) The "who to fight with" resonated deeply now, thinking of Marco.

They explored every inch of each other against the Siren, their bodies becoming one with the ancient art, their passion a timeless ritual. The water enveloped them, muffling the sounds of their ecstasy, creating a private world of unparalleled sensation.

As they finally broke the surface, gasping for air, the sun was setting, painting the sky in fiery hues. They were exhausted, but exhilarated. They had found not just a legend; they had lived it, and Angelina had found a new resolve that went beyond the physical. She felt ready to bring this uninhibited power back to her world, to transform her business with the same courage she'd found in these depths.

Chapter 16: The Beach Bonfire and the Shared Secret

Their adventures were a constant reminder of the boundless possibilities of pleasure, and Angelina found herself embracing a deeper level of exhibitionism, not just for the thrill, but as a natural extension of their uninhibited connection. They reveled in the delicious risk of being seen, the shared secret adding an intoxicating edge to their encounters. This daring freedom, she realized, was reshaping her approach to her life back home; the idea of "fighting alone" now felt less appealing, the thought of trusting others, even with her farm, less daunting.

One evening, Kai organized a private beach bonfire for a small group of his closest, most adventurous friends – a mix of free spirits, artists, and fellow thrill-seekers. The air was filled with the scent of burning wood, grilled fish, and the distant sound of steel drums. Laughter and conversation flowed freely, punctuated by the crackle of the fire and the gentle lapping of the waves. The aroma of rum punch and grilled snapper filled the air, mingling with the salty breeze.

Angelina found herself chatting easily with Kai's friends, sharing stories of her Tuscan farm, speaking with passion about her olive oil, and even about the aggressive competitor. She spoke briefly about the challenges she faced, testing the waters of vulnerability. Their responses, surprisingly supportive and non-judgmental, emboldened her. She found herself truly *connecting*, not just performing, and realizing that perhaps her business didn't need to be so secretive either.

As the night deepened and the champagne flowed, the atmosphere grew more intimate, more liberated. Angelina, wearing a flowing, sheer cover-up over nothing at all, felt a familiar hum of desire building within her. She caught Kai's eye across the fire, a silent invitation passing between them.

He rose, extending his hand to her. "Care for a walk, my love? The moonlight calls."

They strolled along the deserted stretch of beach, the soft sand cool beneath their feet, the moonlight casting a silver glow on the water. The sounds of the bonfire party faded into a distant murmur, leaving them in their own private world.

"I want you, Kai," Angelina whispered, her voice husky with desire. "Here. Now."

Kai's eyes twinkled. "As you wish, my tempest."

He pulled her into the shadows of a cluster of swaying palm trees, barely visible from the bonfire. Without a word, he lifted her, with Angelina wrapping her legs around his waist. She felt his hard erection press against her, already throbbing.

"I want them to know," Angelina breathed, her lips brushing his ear. "Not see, but know. Feel our pleasure in the air. Like an offering to this freedom we've found." The thought solidified her resolve: she wouldn't just trust Marco, she would embrace a bold, public strategy for her brand, a vibrant display of the passion that went into every bottle.

Kai grinned, a wicked glint in his eyes. "Consider it done." His dominant nature found a new expression in this shared exhibitionism.

He entered her with a powerful thrust, Angelina gasping as she wrapped her arms around his neck. He began to move, slowly at first, then with increasing urgency, his hips slamming against hers. The sounds of their lovemaking, soft moans and the rhythmic slap of skin, were barely audible above the gentle rustle of the palm fronds and the distant laughter from the bonfire.

Angelina pressed her face into his neck, biting gently, her body arching into his thrusts. The thrill of being so close to their friends, yet utterly hidden, amplified her pleasure exponentially. She imagined the subtle energy radiating from their hidden spot, a silent testament to their uninhibited passion.

"You're so wet," Kai whispered, his breath hot against her ear. "So tight. They must feel the vibrations in the sand."

Angelina giggled, a breathless, erotic sound. "Let them wonder. Let them feel the heat. Let them feel the power of truly letting go. Of sharing."

As their climax approached, their movements became more frantic, their moans more desperate, yet still hushed, a delicious tension. Angelina cried out, a guttural sound swallowed by the music, her orgasm shattering through her. Kai followed, his own release a deep, shuddering groan. They clung to each other, breathless, their bodies slick with sweat and the lingering scent of sex.

They spent the rest of the night dancing, their bodies still humming with the afterglow, occasionally stealing a touch, a kiss, a knowing glance that spoke volumes of their shared, audacious secret. The full moon rave had been the ultimate canvas for their exhibitionist desires, a night where they truly embraced the wild, uninhibited freedom of the Bahamas. Angelina felt a profound shift within her. The woman who had once guarded her privacy so fiercely was now openly, gloriously, unashamedly herself, ready to trust and to share, even the parts of herself she'd kept most hidden. She knew now how she would fight for her farm: not with secrecy and guardedness, but with bold, unapologetic passion, just like this night.

Chapter 17: The Pirate Shipwreck and the Golden Hour

Kai's fascination with sunken treasures wasn't limited to legends. He was constantly scouting for new wreck sites, his keen diver's eye spotting anomalies in the shifting sands of the ocean floor. One morning, he returned from an early dive, his eyes alight with excitement.

"Angelina," he announced, pulling her into a tight embrace, "I've found it. A true pirate shipwreck. Old, deep, and untouched. And I saw something... gleaming."

Angelina's heart quickened. "Gold?"

Kai winked. "Perhaps. But certainly, something worth exploring. The currents are tricky, so we'll need to time it perfectly. Golden hour, just before sunset, when the light filters down just right." He paused, his gaze thoughtful, a rare moment of introspection for the emotionally guarded man. "You seem lighter today, Angelina. More... resolved. Has our journey helped calm yours? Has it helped you think about that competitor?"

Angelina smiled, a genuine, open smile. "More than you know, Kai. Being here, with you, it's like a different kind of strength is building inside me. Less about control, more about flow. And yes," she added, her voice firm, "I'm starting to think about my farm differently. Marco has really stepped up since I gave him more freedom. Maybe I don't have to fight alone. Maybe there are other ways to win, by being more open, by trusting the team I have."

The anticipation built throughout the day. They prepared their gear meticulously, checking tanks, regulators, and underwater lights. As the sun began its descent, painting the sky in hues of orange and purple, they motored out to the coordinates Kai had marked.

The dive was challenging. The currents were indeed strong, pulling them relentlessly, but Kai's expertise and Angelina's growing skill allowed them to navigate the treacherous waters. As they descended deeper, the light faded, and the ghostly silhouette of an ancient galleon slowly emerged from the gloom.

It was magnificent and haunting; its wooden skeleton draped in centuries of coral growth. Fish darted through its decaying hull, and ancient cannons lay silent on the seabed. Kai pointed to a section of the stern, where a faint, golden glow emanated.

They swam towards it, their hearts pounding with a mixture of awe and excitement. Nestled within a partially collapsed cabin, half-buried in sand, was a small, ornate wooden chest. It was locked, but Kai, with a practiced movement, produced a small crowbar from his gear and pried it open.

Inside, nestled on a bed of faded velvet, were not gold doubloons, but a collection of exquisite, antique sex toys and a beautifully preserved, leather-bound journal filled with explicit drawings and passionate entries from the ship's captain. The "gleaming" Kai had seen was the polished brass of a particularly ornate dildo.

Angelina gasped, her eyes wide with a mixture of shock and delight. "Kai! This is... incredible! A treasure beyond gold!"

Kai chuckled, his eyes crinkling at the corners. "Indeed, my love. A treasure for the truly discerning. For those who seek something more profound than mere currency." He picked up the journal, its pages surprisingly intact. "Imagine the stories these walls could tell. The lives lived, the passions unleashed. The captain, perhaps, found his own kind of freedom down here. A freedom not just for himself but shared with those he trusted." His words echoed his own realization that true freedom comes from choosing vulnerability and shared experiences.

They spent the remaining time in the wreck, not just admiring the artifacts, but using them. In the ghostly light of the sunken ship, surrounded by the silent witnesses of history, they made love, incorporating the antique toys into their play. Angelina found herself utterly aroused by the weight of the past, the thought of the captain and his lovers using these very objects centuries ago. Kai used the brass dildo to tease her, then gently entered her with it, making her moan into her regulator, the sound echoing strangely in the water.

They exchanged deep, lingering kisses, their bodies moving in a slow, sensual dance amidst the decaying grandeur of the shipwreck. The golden light of the setting sun filtered down, casting an ethereal glow on their entwined forms, turning their private pleasure into a sacred, timeless ritual.

As they ascended, leaving the sunken treasure behind, Angelina felt a profound connection to the past, and to Kai, who had brought her to this extraordinary experience. They had found not just gold, but a shared history of desire, and a deeper understanding of the boundless nature of trust, both in pleasure and in life. She felt invigorated, ready to return to Tuscany and implement the bold, open strategies she had envisioned, confident in Marco's capabilities.

Chapter 18: The Full Moon Beach Rave and the Public Display

The Bahamian nights were often alive with impromptu gatherings, but the full moon beach rave was legendary. Word spread through the island's underground network – a clandestine party on a remote stretch of sand, fueled by pulsing electronic music, glowing neon lights, and an atmosphere of uninhibited freedom. Angelina and Kai, always drawn to the most vibrant and liberated experiences, were naturally among the first to arrive.

The beach was transformed into a kaleidoscope of light and sound. Lasers cut through the darkness, painting patterns on the swaying palm trees. The bass throbbed, vibrating through the sand and into their very bones. People danced with wild abandon, their bodies gleaming with sweat and neon paint. The air was thick with the scent of tropical cocktails, marijuana, and raw human energy. The rhythmic pulse of the music, a blend of Soca and electronic beats, was a primal invitation to shed inhibitions.

Angelina, wearing a shimmering, barely-there sequined top and tiny shorts, felt the primal rhythm take hold. Kai, shirtless and glistening, pulled her into the heart of the dancing crowd. Their bodies moved as one, their hips grinding, their hands roaming freely over each other.

"This is exhilarating!" Angelina shouted over the music; her lips close to Kai's ear. "I feel completely alive! Like I can do anything! Like I can face anything!" The thought of her competitor, once a source of dread, now felt like a thrilling challenge. She imagined her new sensual marketing campaign, as bold and uninhibited as this very rave.

Kai's eyes, dark with desire, locked onto hers. "Let's push it, my love. Let's truly embrace the freedom of this night. Let the world see your passion. This is where true freedom lies, Angelina, not just in isolation, but in shared, uninhibited joy." His words directly addressed his own desires, emphasizing the importance of shared vulnerability and boundless expression.

He led her deeper into the crowd, where the bodies were pressed closer, the movements more fluid and uninhibited. In the pulsating darkness, illuminated only by the flashing lights, they began to shed their remaining inhibitions. Angelina's sequined top was discarded; her breasts bare and glistening in the neon glow. Kai's shorts soon followed.

Their naked bodies, slick with sweat, pressed against each other, grinding to the relentless beat of the music. They kissed deeply, their tongues tangling, tasting of wine and raw desire. Angelina wrapped her legs around Kai's waist, and he lifted her, holding her against him as he began to thrust.

The sensation was electrifying. Surrounded by hundreds of dancing bodies, hidden in plain sight by the darkness and the chaos, they made love. Angelina's moans were swallowed by the music, her cries of pleasure lost in the roar of the crowd. The rhythmic thrusts, the feeling of his impressive cock deep inside her, the thrill of their public act –

it all combined into an overwhelming wave of ecstasy.

Kai's hands gripped her ass, pulling her closer, his own grunts of pleasure barely audible. He moved with a primal urgency, his body a blur of motion in the flashing lights. Angelina arched her back, her head thrown back, her bare breasts bouncing with each thrust, her nipples hard and erect.

The crowd around them, lost in their own dances and pleasures, seemed oblivious, or perhaps simply accepting, of the raw sensuality unfolding in their midst. A few nearby dancers, catching glimpses of their entwined forms, exchanged knowing smiles or intensified their own movements, drawn into the collective energy. The anonymity of the rave, the collective surrender to primal urges, created a space where anything felt possible, where public sex was just one more defiant act of freedom on a night of uninhibited expression. Angelina and Kai were just one couple among many, lost in the thrill of getting away with it, fueled by the wild energy of the beach.

As they reached their climax, their bodies tensed, trembling with shared release. Angelina cried out, a guttural sound swallowed by the music, her orgasm shattering through her. Kai followed, his own release, a deep, shuddering groan. They clung to each other, breathless, their bodies slick with sweat and the lingering scent of sex.

They spent the rest of the night dancing, their bodies still humming with the afterglow, occasionally stealing a touch, a kiss, a knowing glance that spoke volumes of their shared, audacious secret. The full moon rave had been the ultimate canvas for their exhibitionist desires, a night where they truly embraced the wild, uninhibited freedom of the Bahamas. Angelina felt a profound shift within her. The woman who had once guarded her privacy so fiercely was now openly, gloriously, unashamedly herself, ready to trust and to share, even the parts of herself she'd kept most hidden. She knew now how she would fight for her farm: not with secrecy and guardedness, but with bold, unapologetic passion.

Chapter 19: The Bittersweet Farewell

As the weeks turned into months, Angelina's time with Kai became a whirlwind of unparalleled passion, exhilarating adventure, and profound self-discovery. He had truly been her catalyst, a force that swept away her inhibitions and showed her depths of desire she had not known before. He taught her to be bold, unapologetic, and utterly free in her sensuality. Their connection, though intense and all-consuming, was always destined to burn bright but briefly. Kai was a creature of the ocean, bound to no land, no person, his thirst for new horizons as boundless as the sea itself. He had once told her of a remote, untouched archipelago he longed to explore, a place even wilder than the Bahamas, where he could continue his ocean exploration and push his endurance. His journey, like hers, was about constant discovery.

As their final days together drew near, a familiar, bittersweet ache began to settle in Angelina's heart. She savored every moment, every touch, every shared laugh, knowing their paths would soon diverge. She understood Kai's nomadic nature, his insatiable thirst for new experiences, and the constant call of the open sea. It was a part of him she admired deeply, even as she yearned for something more rooted, more stable, a connection that could anchor her while still allowing her spirit to soar.

Their parting was not without sadness, a quiet melancholy that settled over their last shared sunset. They sat on the beach, the waves gently lapping at their feet, the sky a canvas of fading purples and oranges. "It feels strange," Angelina admitted, her voice soft, "to know this chapter is closing."

Kai reached for her hand, his callused fingers intertwining with her own. "Every journey has its end, *mia cara*," he said, his voice a low rumble. "But the lessons, the experiences... they stay with you. They become part of who you are." He looked out at the horizon, a wistful expression on his face. "I've always believed freedom was about avoiding deep commitments, about being untethered. But with you, Angelina, I've learned that true freedom can also be found in choosing vulnerability, in trusting someone enough to reveal all aspects of yourself. The deepest adventures aren't always solo journeys." His eyes met hers, a depth of emotion she hadn't seen before. "This connection... it's been profound. It's changed me."

Angelina's eyes welled up, but she smiled through her tears. "And you, my magnificent storm. Thank you for showing me what it truly means to be free. For showing me that trust isn't just about surrender, but about power. The kind of power that lets you ask for help or build something bigger than yourself." She thought of Marco, of the weekly reports filled with his renewed energy and impressive results. The competitor, while still a threat, no longer consumed her with dread. She no longer felt the need to face her business battles alone. She felt a new kind of confidence, a willingness to open her closely guarded world, not just in her personal life, but in her professional one too.

As his boat sailed away, a solitary figure against the vast horizon, Angelina stood on the shore, watching until he was just a speck. She carried the indelible memories of their erotic exploits, the shared laughter, the taste of salt on her skin, and the profound lessons he had taught her about her own desires and her boundless capacity for pleasure. Their relationship had been a powerful catalyst for self-exploration, and she embraced the newfound knowledge of her uninhibited spirit. Kai, too, had learned that the deepest adventures weren't always solo journeys, and that true freedom came from choosing vulnerability with the right person.

In the aftermath of their separation, the vibrant echoes of their Bahamian journey still resonated within her. Yet, amidst the lingering thrill, Angelina found herself craving a deeper connection, a partner who could not only satisfy her physically but also provide the emotional anchor she yearned for. She wanted someone to share not just the thrilling moments but the quiet ones, too—the lazy Sundays, the inside jokes, the shared dreams for a future built on more than just exhilarating escapades. Her experience with Kai had taught her the power of trust, and she realized that this trust, this willingness to open up, could extend to her professional life too. She wouldn't fight alone anymore. In fact, she had already begun to win by embracing collaboration and a bolder vision.

She sought a companion who could truly match her appetite for adventure, who understood her wild spirit, and who would embrace her newfound boldness, not just for a season, but for a lifetime. Angelina knew that her sexual awakening with Kai had set a new standard—one of uninhibited pleasure and mutual satisfaction, but also one that now demanded a deeper, more enduring emotional resonance. Her selective but passionate nature was now seeking a profound, lasting connection.

As she ventured forth from her Bahamian sanctuary, Angelina remained open to the possibilities that lay ahead. She knew that her "forever person" was out there, someone who could offer her the stability she craved while still embracing the adventurous, uninhibited side she had discovered. The Bahamian journey had prepared her, tempered her, and left her ready for the next, perhaps final, chapter of her extraordinary love story, one where she would not only conquer her external challenges but also find a love as rich and complex as her own evolving soul.

The End

The Angelina Novellas

Camille Laurent: Weaving Worlds with AI

The Camille Laurent brand is a groundbreaking fiction writer and AI digital artist redefining the landscape of storytelling and community engagement.

This highly anticipated debut, The Angelina Novellas, is a compelling 7-book series that showcases the ability to blend rich storytelling with cutting-edge technology.

The overarching mission is twofold: to enthrall readers with imaginative and compelling stories, and to inspire a wider audience to explore the exciting possibilities of creating art and prose with artificial intelligence. This work champions the idea that AI is not just a tool, but a powerful partner in unlocking new realms of creative expression.